A BOOK OF SHORT STORIES

Tabitha Potts

Second edition published by Wish Hounds Press 2024.

Cover design by Sophie Harris-Greenslade.

ISBN: 978-1-7385367-0-2

BIOGRAPHY

Tabitha Potts' short stories have been published in various short story anthologies and literary magazines. She recently received an Honourable Mention from the Alpine Fellowship Writing Prize. She has been long-listed for the Royal Academy Pindrop Award and the Sunderland Short Story Award, a Finalist in MIROnline's Folk Tale Festival and Highly Commended in MIROnline's Booker Prize Competition judged by Ian McEwan. She was the winner of the Almasi League Micro-fiction Award judged by Courttia Newland.

Tabitha has a First in English Language and Literature from Oxford University and an MA in Creative Writing. She runs Story Radio, a short story podcast, in her spare time on www.storyradio.org and you can read more stories on her website at www.tabithapotts.com.

DEDICATION

For Jay

CONTENTS

CROW
GIRL

Illustration by Amy Shepheard

CROW GIRL

I was a foundling brat, rescued from the hedgerows where I lay with my beak open, screeching fit to wake the devil. I often think it very likely the first thing I ever saw was a bird in its nest. The people here are thin-mouthed and hard-fisted; you're as likely to get a stone as a piece of bread from them. Still, the Wattses took me in, as they had neither chick nor child. Jonah said to his wife Sally that having another pair of hands would be useful.

As I grew up, I couldn't understand what was being said to me: all I saw was beaks opening and closing. When I tried to speak, people laughed and called me 'Crow Girl'. Jonah and Sally talked to me with gestures, and when that failed, cuffs to the head.

I understood I had to work hard to earn my keep and I became a silent, frightened thing. I learned to read and write a little, from looking at any picture books and papers that I could get my hands on, but I couldn't speak.

My friends were the birds. I spent so much time in the woods with them I knew where they built all their nests, when they arrived in Spring and when they would leave for Winter. The only things I didn't know about them were their songs, but I could recognise every one from a single feather or an egg.

I would feed them whenever I could find food to give them, and some of them got to know me, especially the crows who never forget a human face. I would stand in the woods in my red dress, and the crows would fly to me. I even helped one who had broken his wing, splinting it and nursing him back to health.

Every Autumn there was a fair in a larger village a few miles away. Usually, I didn't get to go but this year Sally sent me as she wanted some lace and ribbons for her clothes. It was the first time I'd been so far away from home. I had a note in my pocket for the lace-maker and the ribbon seller and a few coins in my purse and my heart beat fast as I walked along the highway.

When I reached the fair I was footsore and weary, but I knew I had to find the lace and ribbons before I could look for a place to sleep. There seemed to be hundreds of people, there was the smell of meat cooking which made my belly rumble. There were so many tents decorated in bright colours.

It was hard for me to find the lace-maker, but eventually, I did, and she understood my gestures and the note I gave her. I got three fine collars for a good price. Then I went to look for the ribbon seller.

He was a handsome lad with a free and easy air about him and dark hair and eyes like mine. When I showed him my note he shook his head, he couldn't read. Then he smiled and started showing me his ribbons.

One was pale blue like a robin's egg, soft like down. I nodded. One was dark blue and satin shiny as a jay's feather. I smiled back at him and handed him a coin. Then he took out a scarlet ribbon, as bright as a robin's breast and put it in my hair and gave me a kiss.

With that ribbon, he bound me to him for good, for I was a foolish girl who knew nothing of men.

But I was just a fairing for him, and he was a pedlar after all. I never saw him again after that one night we spent together, warm and happy in the nest we made for ourselves.

When I started showing three months after the fair Sally boxed my ears and told the priest and he told her to throw me out. I wasn't sad to leave the Wattses; I'd never known much kindness under their roof. I knew my friends would look after me.

I moved away from the village, deep into the woods where there was an old cottage. I'd learned how to hunt, fish and forage from all my time alone there and so there was enough food for me and my little egg at first. Then winter came and life was hard for me.

Sometimes Sally came with a loaf of bread or a bottle of beer and some cheese. I think she felt bad for me. Before I got too big, the village men would pay me for an hour or two between my thighs. I didn't care. I only wanted to feed my egg and see it hatch.

When the priest came to see me one night and offered me a coin, I shook my head and held up two fingers. Charged the bastard double. We had a good dinner the next day, the egg and me. I could feel it jumping inside me, stretching its little wings.

At nights I'd curl up by the embers of my fire, banked up with peat, to keep warm. I'd go outside to piss and I'd see an owl hunting for mice, its great white wings making it look like a ghost and the moon above me as bright as a lantern. When it snowed, I put rags in the windows and kept the fire going night and day. It was a hard winter, especially when the men stopped visiting me but by then I had enough coin laid by to keep my egg warm.

I had a hard time of it when I birthed my babe. But Sally came; she must have known it was my time. She helped me cut the cord, wash and feed him – my fledgling was a little boy. The Spring I spent with him was the happiest time of my life. But then the priest came, with men from the village. They said the babe did not belong with me as I was not fit to be his mother. They stole my fledgling from me.

I went the church on Sunday. I stood in the doorway as the priest was opening his beak and

I pointed at him. He looked red and angry and mouthed something at me that might have been 'whore'. Why, he should know, as would half the congregation.

He came out of his wooden box to shout at me, I laughed in his face and then walked out. As I left the churchyard, I saw an old crow watching me and the priest from the gravestone where he was perched. He had a crooked wing and his eyes were bright.

The next Sunday morning, the villagers came to play me some rough music. Of course, I could hear nothing and only realised when I came out of doors to fetch water and saw them standing round the cottage banging their pots and pans and holding a dead crow, wearing a red dress, on a pole. But my friends the crows heard and as I stood in my doorway, clad only in my shift, I saw one perch in the trees around my old cottage.

He was joined by another, and another, and soon the villagers began to slow down, falter, as a thousand black eyes watched them silently. One of them turned tail and fled, and the rest followed him.

The villagers went on to the church to give thanks for their summer harvest, even though they had done this unholy thing. It was there, in the churchyard, that they found the priest lying dead beneath a tree, surrounded by black feathers.

He had scratches covering his face and all over his body, and his eyes had been pecked clean out so all that was left were bloody holes. There was a crow in the churchyard, the one with the crooked wing, but he flew away.

Three days later, when I woke up, I found my fledgling on the doorstep of my cottage, wrapped in a blanket. I never found out how they got him back, or who did it, although I like to think Sally helped. He grew strong and handsome, and we spoke together with a language we invented ourselves.

As he grew older, he would visit the village and eventually he learned to talk like the others too. He married and lives in the village now, but he visits me every few days with my grandchildren.

The villagers call me Crow Girl no longer, but Crow Lady, and come to me for spells and simples.

Every day, I feed my friends. I stand in the door of my cottage and throw crumbs out for them, and they watch me with their bright black eyes.

24 July 2019
This piece came in the Top 5 in The Mechanics' Summer Folk Tale Festival and is reproduced with permission from MIROnline

THE
EDGE

THE EDGE

There's not much to do in the caravan park, and Mum says me and Alannah should go out for a walk, she needs to get on and make our dinner. Alannah's been quiet all afternoon, sulking most likely. She's lying on our bed in the back of the caravan, playing on her phone. I don't mind sharing the room with her normally, we have a laugh, but I'm starting to wish I hadn't invited her to come with us.

'Come on then. Let's go up the cliff.'

'I'm tired. And I've got sunburn.'

She turns over on the bed, her back towards me so I can see how pink she is, and sighs.

'I'll give you some money, Jasmine,' Mum goes. 'You can both get some drinks in that café.'

Usually she doesn't give me money for the café, it's well expensive.

'Let's go then!' says Alannah. She stops being salty with me, just like that. She wants a cool drink sitting outside the café on the hill, just as much as I do.

We'd been on the beach all day. I wore my yellow bikini and Alannah wore her pink one. Pink is to go with her red hair, and yellow suits what she calls my 'olive' skin. We took some selfies of us lying there with the sand between our toes. We'd both painted our fingernails and toenails cherry red, so they glistened in the sun. Alannah's jealous of me because I don't burn. She has to wear factor 50 all the time and sit under a beach umbrella. Still, though, the boys all check her out when she's sitting there in the shade.

That's why it was a surprise when that boy on the beach asked if he could Whatsapp me and not her. He was nice looking and a bit older than us. She was surprised too. She'd been talking about him all week and I suppose she was just expecting him to like her best.

I mean, Alannah's got these big green eyes and long legs. She looks like she's a lot older than thirteen now she's got boobs. I just look the same as ever really, skinny and tall. She used to get called ginger at school, but nowadays it's 'strawberry blonde'.

We've been best mates since my first day at primary school. I arrived a few years later than everyone else, after Mum moved back into Nan's house in Mile End. This tall ginger girl with her hair in plaits came over to me when I was standing there in the playground on my own, eyes all prickly with tears, and asked me to play with her. And just like that, things were OK. I got picked on too sometimes, I'm either too dark or not dark enough, depending on who you ask. It's like my Nan used to say, the nail that sticks up gets hammered down.

We start walking up to the top of the cliff. As usual, Alannah goes on the left, next to the cliff edge and I go on the right. We don't discuss it, she just knows, same way she always sleeps nearest the door because I don't like it. I'm scared that someone might come in. She laughs at me sometimes and says I'm a baby. I don't care.

Sometimes bad things do happen, and I don't like heights.

It's still really hot outside even though it must be getting late and sweat runs down my back as we head up. It's quite a long climb and we don't talk much, because we're saving our breath. The grass is long and dry and it makes a swishing noise as our legs scissor through it. At the top of the cliff, there's a barrier marking off the edge of the cliff from the main bit leading to the café. The sign says 'Cliff fall – do not go beyond this barrier.'

Alannah stops and looks at it like she's never seen it before. 'Let's take another selfie,' she says. Her eyes are glittering like they do when she's excited. She edges around the barrier.

'Don't be dumb.'

'You're so boring, Jas. Boys don't like boring girls. Bet you've never even kissed a boy.'

I can feel the heat rising on my face. She knows I never kissed any boys.

'You're just a boring little baby.'

Slowly, I edge towards the barrier. What I don't like is when I can't see over the edge of something and I don't know what's waiting for me. It means I have to freeze completely still, or go back. I thought I was the only person in the world like this, then I googled it. It's not called vertigo. It's called acrophobia. 'An irrational or extreme fear of heights.'

Alannah's still there waiting with that weird look in her eyes. I creep around the barrier but I'm holding on to it. Now there's only half a metre to what looks like the edge of the cliff, Alannah is so close to it, waiting for me. It's so high up here. Out on the sea, there is a little white boat, sailing along the horizon. If I look behind me, there's no one around. It's just the boat, Alannah and me.

'Oh, you made it! OK, selfie time.'

Alannah turns me around, puts her face next to mine and lines up the shot. I can smell her sweat. She smells of salt. I can see our faces in the little screen, right next to each other, just like the thousands of selfies we've taken over the years, except that in this one neither of us is smiling.

'You don't even like him, do you?' she says. 'You don't like boys much. They scare you.'

'Let me take one,' I say, and she passes me her little pink phone as I'd left mine behind. My stomach is churning. It takes a second and it makes no sound. I imagine our two faces sinking into the dark green water as the phone dies.

15 March 2019
This story was published online by Short Edition as part of a competition.

HAGSTONE

HAGSTONE

The pebbles crunched beneath her feet. She was walking below the dunes, close to the sea's edge. Seaweed lay around, flung into position by the advancing waves. Over towards the horizon she could see the revolving arms of the wind farm, back towards the village of Cley were the marshes and a couple of birdwatchers, intently photographing what looked to her eyes like a very unremarkable flock of tiny brown birds.

It was cold and the sky was a steely grey, a North wind whipped past her from the ocean, lashing up fierce-looking surf. She had prepared herself for cold weather and was wearing a cable knit sweater and a navy blue quilted jacket – sturdy and practical. Now she felt a wave of warmth sweep up her body and little prickles of perspiration started under her arms. She ripped open the jacket, enjoying the cool sensation of the air on her flushed face and neck.

She looked down for a moment, always on the hunt for interesting stones or sea glass. One had a hole in it, so she picked it up: a hagstone. A stone you could look through, and perhaps see another world. Or that could protect you from curses and bad magic. She put it up to her eye and squinted; there were the marshes and village beyond, the church and the old windmill. Her world now.

Sometimes she wondered if buying the cottage had been a mistake. It had been a kind of mania in London: she'd spent hours transfixed in front of her laptop, glass of wine in hand, scouring property sites for isolated cottages, for restoration, somewhere by the sea. She had been on first name terms with rural estate agents, driving many miles around the flat countryside of Norfolk every weekend. She'd come to know the route along the motorway through Thetford Forest very well, the procession of dark pine trees that seemed to continue forever.

But now, as half the proceeds of the house sale were coming to her, was her chance. She had applied for a lecturing position at the university in Norwich when the History department advertised a vacancy and to her delight, she'd got it. She missed her beautiful kitchen in the townhouse in Walthamstow. It had had an Aga, and its old windows had let in the light in a certain way. She missed being married. But the cottage gave her something to look forward to. When she'd seen it on the website, 'needing complete refurbishment and modernisation,' she'd felt a stab of excitement. It felt as though it was hers already, and she'd acquired it with the smoothness and swiftness of a dream.

She stuffed the stone in her jacket pocket and headed back to the car. As she slammed the car door, her phone buzzed. Tony's name came up and her finger paused over the 'Reject' button before she accepted the call.

'Hi. What do you want?'

'I just wanted to say that you should get the Decree Absolute soon.'

'Thanks. I can hardly wait.'

'Margery, please don't be like that...'

There was a sharp intake of breath and she guessed he was smoking. Presumably he'd been sent outside so that the cigarette smoke wouldn't harm the baby. She still couldn't quite believe that Becky, who'd started off as his PHD student, was now going to be the mother of his first child.

To cheer herself up, she pictured Tony, who had always claimed to dislike babies when they were together, shivering on a street corner as he took a drag on his forbidden cigarette. She added an oncoming lorry and a puddle on the road dangerously close to the kerb.

'I still don't understand why you've decided to bury yourself in Norfolk. I'll have a pint.'

The street corner vanished. He was probably at the Stars, a shabby boozer favoured by the English faculty.

'Hardly burying myself. The History Department here is extremely good.'

'But it's so far from your friends. It just seems very drastic.'

'I really don't think that's any of your business.'

There was no way she'd admit to him that that was part of the attraction, once 'their' friends had become 'his and hers'. She hung up on him and started the car.

The drive back to the cottage took about twenty minutes. The sky was still bruised and stormy-looking and as she approached the cottage it began to rain. She loved the way you could see the skies out here but it did mean you were exposed to the wind and weather. The cottage huddled next to one of the water filled, reed-lined trenches used to drain the land, overlooking marshes and beyond that, the dunes and the sea. It was the only building for about five miles and what had sold it to her were the sea views. From the top floor, the only thing you could see was the birds and the blue line of the horizon. Unfortunately, the top floor was more or less uninhabitable at the moment. She had made the downstairs sitting room her temporary bedroom while the builders were up there and the kitchen was usable at the moment, if not what you would call comfortable. They'd be back tomorrow.

The cottage was built along the lines of a simple two up, two down in the flint and brick typical of the region but inside there were old oak beams, an inglenook fireplace with a huge hearth stone and a coffin-hatch to compensate for the very narrow stairs. She'd inherited an old Victorian armchair covered in garish florals which she was planning to reupholster and a pretty old brass bedstead from the cottage's previous owner, along with some hideous wallpaper and bathroom fittings that she was going to rip out as soon as possible. The builders had instructions to retain all historical features and she had made a start on researching the best way to restore the house. It was seventeenth century, at least, her own knowledge would have told her that if the estate agent hadn't. She was a tall woman and had to stoop going through the doorways, but it didn't bother her. If she wanted space, she only had to walk outside.

It was cold now and she set about building a fire, setting up a pyramid of wood and newspaper. As she did so, something further up the chimney caught her eye – a little glint of light behind a loose bit of plaster. Picking up a stick, she gave it an experimental poke. There was a scraping noise, and something fell from inside the chimney and landed on the pile of papers. She knelt down to take a closer look. It was a little grey bottle with a design of an old man with a beard roughly worked into the clay. She shook it, and it rattled. She knew you could discover all kinds of things in these old houses, and put it carefully on the mantelpiece next to the hagstone.

She was eating a tuna sandwich in the armchair next to the fire when she heard a noise. It sounded like a baby crying, and it seemed to come from outside her door. She walked to the door, grabbing a torch and her blue raincoat. The rain was now lashing down and it was dark – no human with any sense would be out in this, but she had to look. Swinging her torch to and fro in the darkness, she jumped when she saw a pair of glowing eyes in the darkness. The torch's beam had picked out a bedraggled young cat, more of a kitten really, standing in front of her cottage. As she was holding the door open, it looked at her for a second and then shot into the kitchen where it jumped up on a chair and sat licking itself clean.

Margery shut the door. Walking to the fridge, she put down a saucer full of milk and another with a bit of tuna. The cat looked at her warily and then walked over, eating and drinking with gusto until the plate was empty. She held out her hand to it and made kissing noises. It ignored her and remained on the chair, but later that night she woke up from confused dreams to find its warm weight across her neck, like a scarf, as it lay sleeping, its little head buried in her hair.

'Where did you find that?' the older builder, John, asked her the next day, as they were discussing the cottage.

'What?'

'The witch's bottle,' he said, taking it down from the mantelpiece.

'Hidden behind the plaster up the chimney. Is that what it is?'

'I've seen one of these once before. People used to use them against witches – you know they believed in them around here.'

She'd read about the witch trials in Great Yarmouth when she'd visited the Tolhouse Gaol where the witches – ten women and one man – were held. Five of them were found guilty and hanged, including Elizabeth Bradwell who was accused by Matthew Hopkins, the Witch-finder General, of bewitching a baby boy so that he 'suffered and languished in great peril.' The museum took the generally accepted line that these poor women were innocent victims of gossip and malice, singled out because they had no wealth or man to protect them or because they were 'cunning women' who knew how to make healing remedies from herbs and plants.

'How did they do that?'

'I'm no expert – but what I heard was that by putting things in the bottle that belonged to you, needles and pins, fingernails and even, you know, body fluids, you'd keep witches away from you.'

She shuddered slightly.

'I've never heard of that. How disgusting. They must have been quite afraid.'

'I'll be very safe here now,' she told the cat after John had gone home. But later that evening it jumped up onto the mantelpiece and knocked the witch bottle down, breaking it in half. She put the pieces away in her kitchen cupboard to fix later. Whatever the contents had been, any liquid had evaporated and all that was left were a few rusty bits of metal.

The electricity went out that night, which she'd been warned about – she planned to get a generator put in. She dug out a book on witchcraft trials from the many boxes of history books she'd brought with her and read it by firelight. Women could be suspected of witchcraft after doing little more than giving someone else a hostile look. Or appearing to them in spectral form, or even in their dreams. An evil intention, it seemed, was all that was needed.

Easy enough to bewitch someone, she thought, if that was all it took. She fell asleep in front of the fire, wrapped in a blanket in the old armchair, the cat purring on her lap. In her dream she was walking through a modern hospital, it seemed to be the Royal London, through a door into a hospital ward. Next to a hospital bed she saw Tony sitting in a chair, and in the bed lay Becky, no baby in sight it but hooked up to IV drips and an ECG monitor. Tony looked tired, gaunt and worried. 'Good,' her dream-self thought. She turned to look at the young woman, and even the sight of the girlish, pretty face, the soft curves and luxuriant golden curls, did not make her feel any pity. These were all the hooks and lures she'd used to lure Margery's husband in. They wouldn't do her much good, now.

It was the ringing of the cottage's landline which woke her up at 3am with the insistence of bad news. It never rang usually and she stood up in a hurry, dropping the cat and blanket to the floor in her rush to reach it. Tony was speaking incoherently to her.

'Slow down,' she said. 'I can't understand you.'

She'd gone, he said. Becky was dead. A pulmonary embolism, a blood clot traveled to her lung, very rare, very sudden. They'd tried to save her but they couldn't.

'The baby?' she asked.

The baby was fine – she was being looked after in the maternity ward. 'Oh my god, Margery, what am I going to do? What on earth am I going to do?'

She stood holding the receiver and spoke to him reassuringly. It was as if the rage, the humiliation and impotent misery had drained out of her leaving her empty and clean as the sky she saw outside the cottage.

Later, she dug a little grave in the garden, and buried the witch bottle in it. Let it stay there for someone else to find one day. She didn't want ever to see it again.

31 December 2018
Elixir magazine

THE
BELLS OF
LONDON
TOWN

THE BELLS OF LONDON TOWN

I am a campanologist. That is to say, a student in the ancient art of ringing church bells. It's been several years since this pastime, I suppose you would call it, entered my life.

It had been a long day in the glass tower in Canary Wharf where I'm based. I've given up telling people what I do for a living as their eyes tend to glaze over with boredom, but yes, I make myself, and my bank, a lot of money.

I had been staring at my screens since 5 a.m. It felt as if I hadn't blinked even once. Come evening, my eyes felt dry and gritty.

"How's it going?" asked Joe Wharton, a trader at a desk immediately adjacent to mine and for whom I have a particular distaste. His smug smile suggested he'd had a good day.

"Not bad," I said, with an equally smug expression, inviting him to guess on my fortunes that day. We both knew how turbulent the markets had been for the past few hours, which meant that profits as well as losses could be amplified quickly. I grabbed my coat and made for the office door before Wharton could press the matter any further and drive a conversation towards our bonus payments, which were due in a month's time. Although I was one of the firm's star traders, he was snapping at my heels and evidently saw me as some kind of competition.

I decided to walk home from Canary Wharf, starting on the Thames path to Limehouse. Sometimes, I would hear echoes of old London as I listened to the tidal slap and suck at the water's edge, though all around me was visual evidence of the 21st century, with its sleek towers, glittering facades and corporate self-promotion.

Leaving the River Thames pathway near the Grapes pub, I decided on an impulse to walk up from Limehouse towards my home in Shoreditch. I liked to walk around London in the evenings, when the shadows softened and changed the appearance of the buildings. Trying out this new route, I cut through the marina and across Commercial Road, and after a short time, heard church bells ringing.

Following the sound of the chimes through Stepney Green, I came to a beautiful old church and yard, incongruous among the modern parks and tower blocks. A solitary raven posed theatrically on top of a graffiti-smeared monument, and beyond the bird there seemed to be no one around. It began to rain – at first a few drops and then suddenly a downpour – so I sheltered in the entrance of the church, which, while well-lit, also appeared to be empty.

The ringing stopped abruptly and a casually-dressed man, clearly not the Vicar, walked out into the nave and caught sight of me standing by the open doors.

"Are you here for the practice?" he asked.

I don't know why I said yes, but I did. I normally only talked to strangers when I was out clubbing, drinking and getting high, but on this occasion, I was intrigued. He asked me to follow him, and soon I was standing in the bell ringing chamber of St Dunstan's, where he invited me to help ring rounds, which was a simple sequence of bells played between treble and tenor.

Arthur, the man who'd just invited me to join him, explained how the system worked. "English bells are not chimed, but rather rung," he said. "Each bell is mounted on a wheel facing upwards and the ringer must rotate the bell in a full circle by pulling a rope."

I have a good ear for music and fast reactions, but it is much harder to ring the bell at the right moment than it initially appears, especially given the physical exertion and precise timing it requires.

We began with ringing a "round" and then embarked on "call-change" ringing, which occurs when the sequence of the bells is altered and the changes are called out. I was only starting to get it right at the end of two hours' fairly constant practice. It suited me; my life as a trader also required fast reactions, with focus and calm under pressure. I knew I'd be able to do it well if I put my mind to it.

In the pub afterwards, Arthur told me more about the ringers. I learned how they played in different churches all over the East End, but this church was a favourite because of the quality of its bells and the fact that they had a peal of ten bells – more than usual.

"St Dunstan's is one of the churches from the nursery rhyme," he said in hushed tones, as if imparting some great secret. "All of the churches in that rhyme are near to or in the old City of London." He leaned a little closer. With his beard and round glasses, he was the sort of person that most would immediately class as eccentric and harmless, with a penchant for real ale and a passion for stamp collecting or bird watching. Arthur's obsession, of course, was bells.

"The Bow bells – at St Mary-le-Bow in Cheapside – were rung as a curfew every evening until the nineteenth century," he continued. "In fact, it was the sound of the Bow Bells that persuaded Dick Whittington to turn around and come back to London. And the bell of Old Bailey refers to the great bell at St Sepulchre without Newgate opposite the Old Bailey, which rung every time a prisoner was executed. Newgate was a prison for debtors and for criminals, which is why the bell's words in the rhyme are, 'When will you pay me?'" He lowered his voice a little. "Bells are the heartbeat of this city. Sometimes I imagine if the bells stopped ringing, the city would stop forever."

Recently I've been working longer and longer. As a trader, it's possible to make a lot of money, but that means routinely taking on a heck of a lot of risk and being in the office all hours. This means I don't have time for much else than work. However, I am bell ringing at least once a week now, usually when the financial markets are closed, and whenever else I can, really.

I don't know why I find my new pastime so satisfying, but I undeniably do. Perhaps I am helping to keep the city's heart beating, or is it the sheer thrill I get from ringing a pitch-perfect peal? Peals are when you are able to ring changes continuously, with a minimum of 5,000 changes. A peal must be "true" in that there must be no repetition of any change throughout. I love the idea that truth and falsity can be so readily determined in bell ringing. I could ring peals all day if I had the time.

My name is now in the peal book at St Leonard's, Shoreditch, where there are 12 bells for "change" ringing. I learned that this was another of the nursery rhyme churches when I saw the letterbox for "Oranges and Lemons letters" whose final destination this is. Shoreditch bells in the nursery rhyme say, "When I grow rich" because the area was so poor; at one point the church had to raise money to build a workhouse for the parish.

It's certainly changed now. My place in Shoreditch cost a fortune. I bought it outright after last year's bonus payment, and in this market, the value can only go up as far as I can see. I definitely see the property as an investment.

There's a girl among the ringers, called Sara. She was talking to me about the spiraling property prices in East London and what it means for locals. Apparently they're getting priced off the market and have to buy cheaper properties farther out. I told her that prices going up will mean more money moving into the area, and eventually it will improve housing stock, schools and retail provision.

Twenty years ago, this area was awful, I told her, and it would have stayed that way if people like her had their way. By that I meant it would have still been full of high crime, unemployment and people living on benefits. She asked me what I did for a living and when I told her, she gave a broad smile. "That makes sense."

She was a lot better looking than you might expect, so I asked if she wanted to join me at my favourite club in London, where the whole dance floor applauds you if you buy a magnum of champagne. She declined. Her loss. She probably would have had the best night out in her life, or at least that's what I told myself. Lately, I've tended to go shopping for women on the Internet. You get to have a good look before you "Buy." There's a huge amount of choice; guaranteed high quality if you don't mind paying the price, and best of all, you can send them back.

Arthur told me that one of the other churches named in the long version of the nursery rhyme, St Botolph's, was in an area infamous for prostitution and it was called the prostitute's church. Old Father Baldpate ring out the slow bells of Aldgate in the rhyme. Old Father Baldpate is a reference to Saint Botolph's tonsure, or possibly something slightly further down his torso. But it all comes back to money. That's what I think the bells of London sing about.

Arthur sees it altogether differently. He believes that ringing church bells bring people together. They were rung to celebrate God, or mark a christening, wedding, or funeral. There were harvest bells and gleaning bells to let you know when to start and finish work. There was a bell to let you know when you were allowed to visit Bedlam, the asylum in Bishopsgate. Bells were supposed to protect you against fire, plague, and the devil, which is why they were rung when someone died, to save their soul.

Things are getting very tense at work. I know the ever-smarmy Wharton is watching me closely and I'm worried he might try and stitch me up for taking on too much risk and keeping it quiet. I know the bank won't care if I cut corners, so long as I make a tidy profit at the end of it all. On the other hand, the bosses will deny all knowledge if

I get it wrong. I'm not the first in this situation and I almost certainly won't be the last. Anyway, despite the massive loss showing on my account, I've got some trading tactics that I know will turn it all around. For sure. After all, I understand the market better than anyone.

It was 4 a.m. and I'd been doing an all-nighter at work trying to sort things out – with the help of a few lines to clear my head – when I heard something unusual. I can recognise the sound of bells, any time of day or night. There aren't too many and my ears are attuned to them. There's so much noise pollution that people say you can only hear the Bow Bells in the City and Shoreditch nowadays.

What I heard was a peal that comprised at least twelve individual bells and had some changes that I just couldn't work out. It was coming from a different direction to all the local bell towers and I couldn't place it. I went for a walk to see where these beautiful, compelling chimes were coming from. It's really not hard to follow the bells once you're accustomed to being guided by your ears. I ended up in a place by the river that I hadn't seen before. It's strange to think I'd been working here for so long and hadn't noticed it. There were hardly any lights on the street, just the dark, still water, and it was so late that I couldn't see much beyond the general outlines of buildings. But the sound of the bells was getting closer all the time.

I get more than my 15 minutes of fame and even find myself on the TV news. Mysterious disappearance of rogue trader. Bank could go under – trader missing. The headlines are many and varied.

When interviewed, Wharton describes me as seeming "ill and preoccupied" when he last saw me. Once they start checking the bank's balance sheet and see the damage done, there is an easy explanation. Some people might think I've ended up on a sunny beach somewhere, grinning over a lurid cocktail. Could have happened – there were plenty of cash withdrawals from my own bank account, as well as a lot of over-spending on the corporate credit card, and perhaps it didn't all go up my nose. Of course the police drag the river for me, but the Thames hugs her secrets tightly and nothing's surfaced so far. What people see when they watch the security camera footage on TV – the last recorded moment of my life – is my walking under and then away from the street light, as though I briefly flicker under its illumination and then am swallowed completely by the darkness of the city around me. I become one with it, as if I have never been anything else.

Police say a search of the area is still underway.

16 October 2016
Brick Lane Tales

THE
DJINN

THE DJINN

Salimah heard the front door slam. Ibrahim had left their house for his early morning shift. Reluctantly, she got out of her bed, shivering slightly as the house was never quite warm enough. Omar and Farihah were still asleep, so she had time to wash and say her dawn prayers before dealing with the children. Drawing back the curtain, she saw that the streetlight was still emitting its sickly glow, while the rest of the street was plunged in darkness. Over the wrought iron fence she could see the churchyard, the gravestones looming masses against the grass. Further away in the distance, Canary Wharf flickered, its sparkling lights adding a incongruously glamorous backdrop to Salimah's immediate surroundings of Victorian terraces, each small front garden signalling the socio-economic background of its inhabitants with unerring accuracy: here, an aspirant box tree in a square metal container, there a defiant multicoloured display of geraniums. Salimah's home said little about her. Even the lightbulbs hung on their flexes with no shades to shield their glare, but the house itself was scrupulously tidy, every surface reflecting back the light like a mirror.

She showered and dressed and then, went to pray. Intoning the familiar words, she felt her mind calm and become still and was halfway through when a noise in the room startled her enough for her heart to pound uncomfortably for a few seconds. Eventually she discovered the source of the noise; the scroll inscribed with verses from the Qur'an that she had hung on the wall had fallen from its hook. Carefully hanging it back up, she made sure it was fastened firmly. A sound from the room the children shared made her go to them. Omar was still fast asleep, but Farihah was up in her cot, gripping the sides and staring at her mother with an intense, questioning gaze. Salimah picked her up, enjoying the feeling of the small, warm body wrapped in hers. She went downstairs with the little girl, leaving Omar to wake by himself and come down.

It was daylight by now and as Omar had not emerged Salimah left Farihah in her highchair for a moment and went upstairs to check on him.

He woke up when she stroked his cheek, but she noticed he felt a little hotter than usual to touch. She sighed. This could mean foregoing her trip to the market and Brick Lane. Standing by the door, while the three year old reluctantly got out of bed, she felt a sudden, icy chill. It was as though someone had opened a window directly behind her; the feeling was so strong she even looked around. Of course, there was nothing there. But she shivered and decided to put on her warmest veil rather than any of the lighter ones she sometimes wore.

A couple of hours later, she was wandering down Whitechapel Market with the two children safely stowed in their pram. Omar still was not his normal lively self and was napping, long eyelashes flat on his cheeks. Passing a stall of fruit and vegetables, jackfruit, okra and bunches of herbs, Salimah found herself transported for a moment back home as she inhaled the distinctive warm tang of coriander. She was in the kitchen, holding onto her mother's bright sari while her mother prepared supper, her hands stained with intricate patterns of henna as she chopped the herbs with expert speed. And then she was back on the windswept street where for a moment even the beloved faces of her children seemed unfamiliar, the faces of strangers, part of a life that might easily not have been hers. Salimah was officially not the 'pretty one,' that honour had belonged to Asna, whose luminous skin and whose eyes, large, limpid and richly fringed like the sleeping Omar's, had always seemed fit for a Bollywood star. Salimah's mother had whispered to her once: 'Someone will always watch over you, my darling.' But Asna married young and went to England, their mother died, and Salimah was left at home.

'Salamu Alaykum, what do you want today?' asked the stall holder in Bangla.

Salimah bought two bunches of coriander and some chillis and hung the striped shopping bag over the handles of the pram. Omar woke up and started whining as he had spotted the ice cream shop next to Whitechapel station. Wearily, Salimah steered the pram away.

'1, 2. 1, 2. Bethnal Green? Anyone going to Bethnal Green? You got a bleeding heart, love? Is your heart bleeding?' came the disembodied voice of the office manager. White noise.

'Oh shut up.' Sheila on reception.

'76 I got something for you. Can you hear me 76?'

Ibrahim switched off the radio. He wasn't going to Bethnal Green, he was going home. The night had begun on Brick Lane with four noisy City boys wanting to be ferried from the curry house they were gracing with their presence to a strip joint in Hoxton. They had only tipped a pound, despite the fact that one of them had been sick in the back of the cab. The night continued with a drunken set of Rag Week students dressed as Alice in Wonderlands and Ronald McDonalds. One of the Ronalds was unable to remember where he lived, so Ibrahim had had to cross the Mile End Road three times. The scent of pine from the air freshener hanging in the front of the cab and the smell of vomit from the back seat mixed with the strident perfume of the Alices had made his head ache. As he didn't drink, the boredom of listening to the rambling chat from the back seat intensified his exhaustion – it was now 3.30 a.m. – but it was at last time to go home.

He found a spot for the cab outside the front door of the house. Meticulously tidy as always, he took his cleaning kit out of the back of the cab to replenish the air fresheners and tissues. He was startled to see Salimah sitting at the kitchen table in her nightgown and overcoat. All the lights were on.

'Salamu Alaykum. What's wrong?'

'It's happened again.' Ibrahim sighed.

'What's happened this time?'

Under the harsh lighting the whites of her eyes looked sore and her mouth looked pinched. The photograph of their wedding day back in the village was still on display on the windowsill. Salimah was dressed in her red and gold wedding sari, her usually solemn face smiling up at him. This morning she seemed very different to that young girl, yet it had only been four years since he had married her and brought her here.

'I cleaned the kitchen and then I was making some chicken – the one you like with spinach – while the children were taking their nap. I had my back to the storage cupboards and I was quite busy, you know, chopping up the onions. Then suddenly there was this loud noise, the doors of two of the cupboards opened behind me and everything fell out, the flour and the chickpeas landed on the door and made it all dirty again. And I feel cold. I've been feeling cold all day.'

Her hands were wrapped up inside the overcoat. Ibrahim went over to the cupboards and examined the shelves. She had tidied up but he could imagine an explosion of flour and mess. Nothing seemed to be near the edge of the shelves, and everything was safely in its box or packet. He looked under the stairs for his tools and checked the shelves with a spirit level, as he had done before. No, the shelves were not crooked in anyway. The units were cheap but fairly new. He shook his head.

'I can't see anything wrong. Are you sure you hadn't left something on the edge?'

'I'm sure!'

She was close to tears; he could hear it in her voice. He shivered. All this superstition was getting to him. He didn't need this, he wanted to sleep.

'I only feel peace when I am in the garden.'

Salimah's garden at the back of the house looked bleak now but in summer it would be bright with tier upon tier of chillis, squash and spinach, tomatoes and beans trained up canes and trellis. She had learned how to handle the sticky and dense London soil and grow the plants she remembered from home. The children and the garden were what made her happy, he thought, and felt another wave of irritation.

***

Asna offered Salimah another samosa but Salimah shook her head.

'Acha. You're looking too thin.'

'I can't eat much. I feel ill all the time. The only time I feel better is if I stay away from the house.'

Asna looked across the room at the children playing. She was proud of the lounge; she had had it decorated in a pale pink and it looked out onto a well-kept patio garden. Her eldest boy was showing Omar his toy collection, while

Farihah was playing with the tea-set that Asna had got out for her. Her teenage daughter was too grown up for it now.

'Have you been to see the doctor?'

'I tell him about the chills I've been getting but he can't find anything wrong with me. He says I'm depressed and wants to give me pills.'

' You don't think... he could be right?'

'You've felt it. When you came around the other day you said you could feel how cold it was downstairs. And then you lost your purse.'

'I'm always losing it!'

'You said you'd put it in the kitchen, and it wasn't there. Why would you have left it in the bedroom? You didn't go in there.'

'The kids must have moved it.'

'I know there's something going on. I can feel it.'

'What did the Imam say?'

'He said some holy verses to make it go away. But it isn't gone. You know why I think that is?' 'You tell me.'

'It's something to do with that graveyard. I went to the council and asked us if they could help us find somewhere different to live, but it's going to take a long time.'

Asna watched Salimah, who was slumped in her armchair and staring at the door. It was difficult; they had spent so long apart. She had left as a seventeen-year-old bride when her sister was just eleven. So many years when they could only talk on the telephone, miles apart, when they could have been together. Not enough visits back home, not enough to assuage the ache of missing her mother, not enough to keep her going through the grief after her mother died. Asna was proud of her marriage and her husband who now ran three successful shops, her stylish house and her kids. Her eldest daughter was at secondary school now and doing really well, and her boy was good at maths like his father. She wanted the same things for her sister.

'What does Ibrahim say?'

'Oh, he's working every night, I hardly see him and he's so tired. I think he is angry with me.'

The Curate was busy putting his notes together to prepare for the latest local history walk he was leading that Saturday. He loved to explore architecture, the traces of life lived hundreds of years ago that still survived unacknowledged in the modern chaos of the city. He loved the city farm, with its collection of hardy-looking Gloucester Old Spots, and went there often to visit the ruins of a mediaeval monastery that sat there unnoticed and unvisited except by a herd of athletic miniature goats. He would personally scrub away sprayed-on tags proclaiming the might and dominance of the Stepney Massive, or the same sort of graffiti he remembered from his own school days in Surrey, differing only in the types of names and the breadth of knowledge and inventiveness of the sexual techniques described, when they appeared on the walls of his beautiful church. He felt a thrill of pleasure when he looked around the stone building that sheltered his flock as it had done for centuries, withstanding even the Blitz. It had been a bit of luck to get a challenging, inner city parish, that had a church at its centre as old and beautiful as this. The Curate knew God didn't care about architecture, but was honest enough to admit to himself that he did.

The Curate's latest walk would start on Cable Street. He would explore the Ratcliffe Highway, where sailors from all over the world could once buy wild beasts of all descriptions, from lions and hyaenas to parakeets, moving on to the boundary stone marking the borough of Ratcliffe or 'Sailortown' notorious for its taverns, drug dens, brothels and general debauchery for hundreds of years. He would show them Stepney Causeway, where Dr Barnardo asked that one of the doors be kept permanently open after one child came looking for shelter, was turned away and died two days later of starvation on the streets. He thought how a historical distance could make a world where anything or anyone could be bought and sold and life itself was cheap seem exotic and fascinating while in fact the reality must have been – and was still – terrifying.

The Rector approached him as he was rearranging his notes.

'I have something interesting for you, Andrew,' he said cheerily. 'An infestation, you might say.'

'An infestation?' Andrew, a serious man, had never understood the Rector's donnish mixture of learning and levity.

'A supernatural infestation. A young lady who lives in one of the old houses over there.' He gestured towards the row of Victorian terraces opposite the graveyard.

'She has what appears to be a djinn problem. They're more common than you might imagine.'

'A djinn?'

'It's the same as the word for a genie, but it's not really a case of Scheherazade, Aladdin, rubbing the lamp and three wishes. This is something more complicated, like a spirit that can do good or evil. She believes it is a Christian djinn, or ghost, or whatever you want to call it. You can come with me when we go to see her.'

'Isn't this more likely to be a case of something psychological?'

The Rector sighed.

'Of course that's something to consider. But in this case, if it will ease the anxiety of someone in our parish it is seen as worthwhile to say a few prayers of protection or peace, bless the house, that kind of thing. Deliverance, we call it. Besides, what is psychological, and what is not?'

'I don't follow you.'

'Non-believers would have us locate everything that does not fit into their scheme of things in the human imagination. "The sleep of reason produces monsters", as it says in the wonderful etching by Goya. But if you are willing to accept the possibility of an immortal, why not a monster, too? The Islamic belief is that djinns or genies are a separate part of creation, neither angels nor humans but beings created from fire and possessing free will, so capable of both good and evil. In the Judaeo-Christian tradition there are references to creatures similar to genies, too, the Mazikeen, who were children of Adam. These are centuries-old beliefs.'

'This confirms me in my belief that practical religion is a lot more straightforward than theoretical.'

The Rector smiled at him.

'Well, Andrew, in this case we'll be doing a little of both.'

At Salimah's house, the Rector introduced Andrew to the two women. Salimah had opened the door very swiftly, as though she had been watching out for them.

'My husband doesn't know you are coming here,' she said.

'He doesn't approve of all this, he thinks I am imagining things.'

She gestured vaguely, her hand taking in the small hallway and the stairs. They went to sit down in the front room, directly overlooking the graveyard. 'What will you do?' Asna asked. 'I will say a few words, in each room. I will be asking for a blessing, and protection, on the house and its inhabitants. You do not have to join in the prayers, but we will both give responses. You can remain silent, if you wish.' The Rector smiled kindly at the two sisters, Asna in smart salwar kameez and a bright headscarf, Salimah more dishevelled, as though the high standards of housekeeping apparent around them did not extend to her own appearance. He stood up and started speaking. There was no preamble, no book or candle. The Curate listened to the words and hoped that they would bring the listeners some reassurance.

'Visit, Lord, we pray, this place and drive far from it all the snares of the enemy.'

They continued from room to room, the small procession seeming overly large in the little house. The Curate admired the garden from the hallway window. 'Let your holy angels dwell here to keep us in peace, and may your blessing be upon it ever more; through Jesus Christ our Lord.' It was in the children's upstairs bedroom that all of a sudden the Curate smelt it. It was a terrible stench, something with such an intensity of decay and horror in it that he almost gagged and rushed to the window.

'What is it?'

'You smell it, too?' asked Salimah.

'I can't smell a thing' said Asna. She was staring at him.

'It's horrible! Have you got mice, or rats? I've never...' As he struggled with the old sash window, the smell disappeared.

'It's gone!'

Salimah shrugged. 'That's how it is, I smell it, my boy smells it. The little one, I don't know, but she wakes up at night sometimes screaming in her cot. My husband can't smell anything. I've done everything I can, I keep all the food hidden away, the council says there's no mice, there isn't anything.'

She sounded weary rather than afraid. The Curate noticed for the first time that there were cans of air freshener in every room. The Rector looked at both the women.

'Excuse me. Shall we continue?'

Salimah was finding it hard to sleep after getting Farihah to settle down. She had tried taking the little girl into her own bed at first but it had not comforted her. None of the household had had much sleep for the last few nights and she had tried teething gel and painkillers in case that was what was causing the problem but it didn't seem to help. Farihah would be upright in her cot, shrieking and shrieking with real fear on her face. 'Night terrors,' Asna would tell Salimah on the phone. But Salimah found that after one of these night-time episodes she would lie awake for what seemed like hours, staring at the cracks in the ceiling or watching shapes form and then disappear again in the patterns of the net curtains.

She heard Ibrahim's key turn in the lock. She knew his movements as well as her own. He went to the kitchen to put away his things and she heard him clattering about, opening and closing the cupboards. Then he came upstairs and went to the bathroom where she heard him washing. However, after that there was silence. Normally, at this point he would go to say his early morning prayers. Salimah got out of bed, wrapped a shawl around herself and went to look for him. The house was empty. She rang his mobile in panic. 'Where are you?' She told him what she had heard. He sounded sleepy. 'I'm coming home. I just finished my shift. Don't be silly, there's nothing to be afraid of.' 'It sounded as though someone else came into the house.' 'Well, no one did, you said the house was empty. Look, I'll be home soon, alright?' He cut off the call. Ibrahim's presence once he was finally home in bed, his back turned to her and his eyes firmly closed, wasn't as reassuring as she had hoped.

Later, deep in sleep, Salimah awoke in confusion and terror with Ibrahim's hands fastened tightly around her neck. She wanted to cry out, but couldn't. It was like the worst sort of dream, but the pain and fear told her she was awake. Why were his hands so cold? His eyes were open but seemed glazed, not like those of the man she knew. The sense of something evil in the room was very strong now, so strong that Salimah could almost see it. His hands were tightening and Salimah was about to pass out, but she could see her mother's face flash brightly before her eyes. 'There will always be someone watching over you.'

With a huge effort she managed to get her hands up to his and pulled at his fingers, pulling them back until his hands loosened their grip for a second, enough for her to pull her upper body from under his and then, kicking and scratching in terror, roll from the bed onto the floor. He got up and started walking towards her, his eyes still with that absent and terrifying stare.

***

Andrew found Salimah outside the church as he was locking up after the morning service. She was standing looking at the stained-glass window. She smiled at him.

'It's beautiful. I've never really looked at it properly although I used to walk through the churchyard all the time.'

'How are you?'

'Much better. I wanted to come and say thank you for your help. I'm staying with Asna now, with my children.'

'And your husband?' A shadow passed over her face.

'He has moved away from us now. He is living with his brother. I had to hit him with the bedside lamp, when the djinn took him over. I told the police he was sleepwalking because he'd been sleeping so badly. He didn't believe in the djinn, but it came to him.'

'I want to show you something. I only found this out recently, when I was researching for the history walk and came across a book about crime in the East End of London.' He walked with her over to a grave that stood by itself at the edge of the churchyard. 'The occupant of this grave was originally intended to be a Mr Samuel Reed, a surgical instrument maker. He was a regular churchgoer and lived alone. He was discovered as a suicide in 1810 – he had hanged himself. A letter was found among his effects that confessed to the murder of a young woman ten years previously. The worst of this was that the body of his poor victim, a Miss

Lizzy Barnes, who was identified by a locket he had kept among his papers, had been buried in his own home, under the floorboards.'

'Who was she?' asked Salimah, her eyes on the grave, where little could be seen except the name and the date, 1800. The inscription read simply 'May She Rest in Peace'.

'She was of uncertain occupation, and may have been what they called in those days a fallen woman, or a woman looking for work as a maid or housekeeper, it's hard to tell. He did not explain why he killed her in his letter, only spoke of "a need and compulsion so strong that it took hold of my mind, despite all efforts to tame it through prayer and good works. A need so strong that I almost fear it will outlive me." His confession asked that his victim be given a Christian burial in the plot that he had reserved for himself, where we are standing. He also asked forgiveness for his crime. His own body, as he was a self-confessed murderer and a suicide, was buried with a stake through his heart at a crossroad on Ratcliffe Highway'.

'Where did he live?' said Salimah, still looking at the gravestone.

The Curate pointed towards the row of Victorian terraced houses where Salimah's old house stood, now with metal shutters on the windows while the council found a new tenant.

'There.'

Salimah took a break after she had finished weeding the raised beds in the city farm and went to sit in the arbour she had created above the bench. All around her she could see the fruits of her work: squash whose ripe, plump flesh seemed to invite touching, bright chillis, plump aubergines with purple skins, okra, spinach plants. All around her was beauty, calm and order. In the distance a cock crowed. Salimah herself was no longer thin and pinched, her skin glowed with health and her eyes shone. Sitting by herself in the garden, she thought: now I am home. Now I can live in peace.

15 July 2010
33 East

THE
GIFT

THE GIFT

I had to get a gift for my wife (who is easily disappointed) and I had to get it by 6pm on a cold and rainy Tuesday in London. She demands from me a certain quality in my gifts: they cannot be simply a proof of financial outlay (too crude, too straightforward) nor should they be clumsy, handcrafted love tokens (these are for children and young lovers) but they need to show an insight into her character, display a certain subtlety and a level of intellectual involvement.

As you can imagine, this did not fit well into the timeframe of a business trip, but my stay had been unexpectedly lengthened due to cancellations (a weekend of storms with old fashioned British names such as "Storm Archie") and I now had some time to solve the problem. Not the problem of my wife (if only such a solution existed) but the problem of her gift. I had one afternoon.

I took the Underground to East London where my guidebook reliably informed me there was a 'chic' shopping area. I thought this might potentially sell something my wife would tolerate or even, perhaps appreciate (so different from her attitude to me). There is something about the rain in London which is unique. I'd hardly ever seen the city without a leaden grey sky accompanied by a light, intermittent rain which slowly dampens your shoes and collar and goes down the back of your neck. I experience rain so rarely in California that it is a novelty, it has a certain noir quality which makes me imagine hearing a distant saxophone, maybe the soft beat of a snare drum.

The streets were dark and narrow, and the buildings were old, not quaint but old old, as though they were about to fall apart, with narrow sidewalks and graffiti. I eventually found an indoor market, which looked as though it had been there for centuries, and walked around the little stalls, but I couldn't find what I needed. I'd more or less given up, and was wondering whether I should go to a more upscale neighborhood, perhaps visit Harrods or Liberty, when I found myself in a street of very old houses, one of which had what looked like an oil lamp flickering outside. Here, I found a little alleyway called Folgate Mews, and curiosity made me look into it. There were more houses, tiny this time, and a shop. Above it a sign painted in gold read 'Apothecary'. Through the glass windows I could see old wooden cabinets with many drawers, a round table covered in small glass bottles, a purple chaise and a long counter. I opened the door, which set a bell chiming, and walked in, ducking my head below the lintel.

Appropriately enough, this very feminine appearing space was inhabited by a charming young woman, who emerged from the shadows behind the counter. She had a porcelain quality, her skin smooth, even and pale, her eyes large and blue and her hair hanging in soft ringlets down her back. The second thing I noticed was a particularly delightful scent: it was hard to identify the source, but eventually I realized it was coming from the candles that flickered above the fireplace in which a log fire was burning. The scent was clean, calm and rather soothing; I detected a note of clean, ironed laundry, lemon and vanilla pods and flashed on a childhood memory: my mother ironing while a cake was baking in the oven, me sitting at the kitchen table, drumming my heels on the chair while doing homework, she humming to herself as she completed her chores. Unexpectedly I found myself tearing up. That had been a moment of pure happiness, hadn't it? How often do those occur?

The elfin creature behind the counter was watching me.

'You like the candles?' she enquired.

'It's very subtle, but it's so... powerful at the same time.'

'You can buy this as a room fragrance, and of course a perfume as well. It tends to be different, for different people. When I smell it, it reminds me of playing in a garden when I was a girl; lavender, roses and a note of mown grass.'

'What do you call it?'

'This one we call Revenir. It's exclusive to our shop. We have many fragrances you may enjoy.'

I couldn't place her accent – European, certainly, but where? There was a delightful low note to her voice, it was enchanting. I could have listened to her all day.

A moment later, I found myself looking at a glittering row of bottles, jars and other small containers that she had spirited onto the counter. There were many different colors, a turquoise that reminded me of Navajo jewelry, an amber of the hue of a cat's eye, one that sparkled with gold flecks and brought to mind a Venetian paperweight that sat on my desk at home.

''We have perfumes for every person. Anything you might desire. This one,' she gestured towards a small, dark red bottle, 'smells of blood.'

I muttered something about not knowing any vampires personally, and she laughed.

'This one,'– a bullet shaped container in a leaden grey color – 'smells of metal and gunpowder. Our clients who wear it say it makes them feel strong and powerful. Mostly men, but more women than you might expect. This one,' she gestured, 'has a top note of smoke, like cigarette smoke, and in the base note you will smell the scent of skin and sweat. It's as though you are in the arms of your lover, lying in bed.'

I looked at the bottle, which was of iridescent silver glass. It had swirls of darker color inside it, which almost looked as though they were moving.

'I don't smoke,' I said, slightly uncomfortably.

'You are looking for something for yourself, or for someone special?' she asked.

'A birthday gift for my wife.'

'Ah. Then I suggest you choose from these three.'

She pushed three little containers towards me on the counter.

'This,' she pointed at a translucent green glass bottle, 'suggests the scents of spring. Floral top notes, base notes of sandalwood, it's fresh and enticing. Your wife will feel, and look, rejuvenated when she wears it. This one,' – a larger, red bottle with golden detailing – 'is full of passion and romance. It has tuberose heart notes, a touch of musk and magical top notes that will entrance everyone around her.'

'What about that one?' It was the plainest of the three, but the color was alluring, a deep, dark purple.

'This is a riskier choice. It is a dark and powerful perfume. We call it Manifest, because it will bring the wearer her most secret desire.'

The bell chimed behind me five minutes later as I closed the door, the bottle of perfume (which had been even more costly than I had expected) nestling in a purple and golden velvet box in my pocket.

I arrived home after a lengthy flight from London Heathrow via Los Angeles International to San Jose and an equally long cab journey with a crazed driver who drove alarmingly fast while telling me about how his ex-girlfriend had pulled a gun on him one night. I was exhausted. Luckily my wife was not home yet; I took a shower, shaved and changed my clothes.

When I came downstairs she was waiting in the kitchen. Our home, in the mountains just outside

San Luis Obispo, overlooked the city below. The light from the low evening sun caught my wife's blonde hair through our wide glass windows, giving her a fiery halo. She'd put two glasses of chilled Sauvignon from our favorite winery on the table. I remembered visiting it for the first time together and how we had exclaimed over the grand building, its formal gardens with their Koi carp lazing through the glassy ponds and then, exploring further, found an airfield where a pilot took us for a short flight in an old fashioned biplane. I remembered soaring through the achingly blue Californian sky with her, her hair lit gold like today, and how we had felt as though we could overcome anything.

Then she found out about my affair and then she miscarried our baby. The two things were separate but it didn't feel like that at the time. That's what she told me.

We exchanged our news – she'd been particularly busy at work, I told her about my trip. Then I handed over my gift. I almost expected the box to be empty when she opened it, like it happens in those old stories my mother read to me as a child – the hero falls asleep clutching fairy gold, only to wake up with a handful of dead leaves. But the squat purple bottle was still there, nestling on its velvet cushion.

She opened the bottle. The scent filled the air: seductive, potent and terrible.

10 October 2010
Mechanics' Institute Review Online

Printed in Great Britain
by Amazon

51417229R00051